FRONTISPIECE.

page 4.

DEAF & DUMB.

"Pray come to us when you take your ride."

DEAF

AND

DUMB!

BY THE AUTHOR OF

" *THE TWIN SISTERS,*" &c. &c.

" That good diffus'd, may more abundant grow,
And speech may praise the Power that bids it flow."

Cowper.

SECOND EDITION.

LONDON:

PRINTED FOR DARTON, HARVEY, AND DARTON,
No. 55, Gracechurch-street.

1813.

PREFACE.

IT is hoped the title of the following book will excite attention: how much more, then, should the unhappy situation of those who are in that state demand compassion! and it is gratefully acknowledged, that in some benevolent minds the tide of pity has flowed even to them. An Asylum, on a plan more and more extensive, as the means of making it so has increased, has been formed for these *once* melancholy appellants to their commiseration, but who are *now*, through their means, enabled cheerfully to pass through life; and scarcely to feel the deprivation of those powers, which, were it not for this institution, would have sunk them into listless apathy, or moody ideotism.

Perhaps the reader is little aware how many of his fellow-creatures are labouring under this misfortune, and how much the number of those who cannot, from want of room, or means for their support, be admitted into the Asylum, exceeds those who have received the benefit of it. Let the following extract acquaint them with it:—"The unhappy malady which affects these

these children is found to exist to a dreadful extent; scarcely a week passes without some application for admission, and though the number of pupils has been gradually augmented from six to sixty, it must be stated (and it is stated with deep concern) that at every election, the *number of candidates* exceeds, in a *tenfold proportion*, the number of vacancies! Such a painful fact makes a most interesting and powerful appeal to every benevolent mind." Another powerful plea may also be added: that, after fourteen, the age appointed by the committee, they cannot be be admitted. Arrived at these years, any one possessing all his faculties, (and who has till then been brought up in comparative ignorance,) finds it difficult to learn. But to these unhappy children, the difficulty must of necessity be increased; besides the danger there is that, if till that time, they are taught *nothing*, it will be beyond the reach of human means to rescue them from the state above described.

The writer of the following pages earnestly appeals to the lively feelings of youth, (the season of compassion,) to consider these things. Let them

remember,

remember, it is for those of their own age that their assistance is demanded; and who, instead of having to look forward to a life of activity and usefulness—or that they shall fill up their place in society beneficially, either to themselves or others, must, without the improvement afforded them by these means, drag on a miserable existence—a burden to themselves and all around them. The necessitous in more advanced life, have, at least, the consolation of thinking every year that passes brings them nearer to the end of their sorrows; and *blessed* are they, if they have a *well-grounded* hope

hope of happiness in eternity. Their troubles then are nothing; but these poor children are not only suffering want at the present, (for it is for the children of *the poor* I plead,) but continuing as they are, they have no prospect of ever raising themselves, by useful industry, above it. And what is still worse, they are in this state excluded from those *means* which are appointed by Divine Wisdom for the instruction of his people, and which lifts their minds to higher veiws, and enables them to support affliction, by acquainting them with another and a better world.

DEAF

DEAF AND DUMB!

"WE are going out in a cart," said Henry Rawlinson, as he jumped down the steps of the street door, to meet Mr. Beaufort, a gentleman who was then on a visit to his father, and who had gained the affections of all the children he was acquainted with, by his kindness to them. "Dear Mr. Beaufort, do you know where we are going?" continued he: "to nurse's house, the woman who nursed me; we are to spend the whole day there." Then taking his hand, he begged him to accompany him into

 the

the yard, to see the vehicle that was to convey them: "It is such a very nice cart," said he, "it is open at the top: won't it be pleasant to ride in it?" "Very pleasant indeed," replied his good friend, smiling to see him so happy; "and who is to be of the party? I fear there would not be room for *me*, should *I* wish to join it," added he, on seeing the neat little cart they were going in. "Why, I think," replied the little boy, in a lower tone, "that you would not like to ride with the servants, not but that they are very good to us. There are Miller, and Sally, and my sister Caroline, and myself; and nurse's son drives us. Do you think there will be room for you?" added he, with an enquiring look,

look. "I believe not," answered Mr. Beaufort; "and besides, my weight, added to all yours, would be too much for the poor horse. But suppose I ride over in the course of the day, and see how you get on; and then I can take you up before me, and we can ride a little way together." "Oh, do, do!" exclaimed Henry, skipping for joy, "I shall be *so* glad; and as for the road, if you don't know it, nurse's son can tell you *that*."

While they were thus settling this pleasurable scheme, the horse and cart were gone round to the door, and "Master Henry" was loudly called for. Mr. Beaufort accompanied him back again, and Henry introduced him to nurse's son, that he might understand the road he was to come to them. "You *cannot* mistake it now," said Henry, on hearing it accurately described; "I hope you'll come."

"What," said Caroline, who was a year or two older than her brother, and who was already seated in the cart, "does Mr. Beaufort talk of coming to us? O! pray do, Sir; you cannot think what a pleasant place it is." "I won't promise," answered the good-natured man, pleased at their eagerness, "but perhaps I may;" and then kindly assisting the servants to get up, he had the pleasure of setting off the whole party, rewarded by their smiles and thanks. "Pray come to us when you take your ride," was loudly re-

peated

peated, both by Caroline and Henry, till they were out of his sight, and, with a look of kindness, he gave them, what they considered, a nod of assent.

Mr. and Mrs. Rawlinson were not up when their children left the house, and had not Mr. Beaufort been an early riser, he would have lost the satisfaction he felt on seeing their happy faces, as it was not quite six o'clock when they commenced their journey. He had the pleasure of describing them to their parents, whom he met at breakfast, and they were equally delighted at the recital. He also mentioned the invitation he had received to pay them a visit some time in the day, and Mr. Rawlinson earnestly seconded it: "Do," said he, "for it is just by the spot on which I wish you to build; and, were I not particularly engaged this morning, I would accompany you." This was *one* inducement to Mr. Beaufort, as he had long talked of building a residence for himself in that neighbourood; and the idea of giving the children pleasure was *another*. He therefore ordered his horse at the usual time, and determined to comply with their request.

In the mean while, the happy party arrived at nurse Goldsmith's cottage, highly pleased with their ride and the kind reception they were sure to meet with. It was between four and five miles from the town, and situated on the side of a

common,

common, part of which belonged to Mr. Rawlinson's estate, and on which he had formed several plantations of firs. Before the house was a neat little garden, sheltered from the north wind by a small coppice of hazel trees, through which ran a murmuring brook, that supplied the family with water. The good woman, with all her children, was at the wicket gate to receive her guests; and all who *could* speak, expressed pleasure at seeing them. But, alas! *all* could not, for two of them were deaf and dumb!

Do my young readers fully consider the extent of this misfortune? and are they truly sensible of the blessings of speech and hearing? Oh, what a pity that they should ever

ever misapply the gift of speech, in murmuring and complaints, because they have not always every thing they wish; or in that which is still more wrong, speaking of the faults of others, or in telling untruths.

Having never heard the sound of the human voice, nor indeed any sound at all, these poor children could not frame their mouths to speak; they could never add to the pleasure of their parents, by repeating what gave pleasure to themselves; nor could they speak their wishes, or their simple thanks, when they were complied with. Let the little ones who read this tale, reflect upon what it is that makes them in any measure agreeable to others. Is it not their conversation? and do they not

not express themselves, as they think will be most likely to induce their friends to comply with their request, whenever they have a favour to ask of them? Alas! those children who labour under the misfortune here described, have no such power; and many such, I am sorry to add, there are! What, then, is the reply of the benevolent heart?—"It is our duty to speak for them, to alleviate their distress, as much as possible, and, if in our power, to contribute to the removal of it." I hope this is the language of all my readers. It has been (and I have seen it with pleasure) that of not a few children, who, on hearing of the Asylum for those of their own age that are thus unfortunate, where they

they are taught to speak, and to understand others, have contributed their small donations; while some, even by a penny a week, collected from a number, have, within a few months, added no inconsiderable sum to the fund which is raised for the support of this charity; and their pleasure is increased by it, in proportion as the gratification of contributing to the relief of such distress, is superior to that obtained by toys or sweetmeats.

Caroline and Henry were soon out of the cart, and greeted with an affectionate kiss from Mrs. Goldsmith; particularly the latter, who returned her caresses with equal affection. He then shook hands with his foster brother, who had been named

named after him, and began asking after the health of some rabbits he had left in his care, while Caroline offered a present she had brought for the eldest girl. She spake to all the rest; but William and Lucy, one ten, and the other five years old, stood on one side. Caroline took the hand of the eldest, and would have kissed little Lucy, but feared distressing her, as she could not recollect her former visits to them. The poor mother's eyes bore witness that she felt her kindness to the unfortunate child: "It is of no use to tell her who you are, Miss," said she, "or I know she would not be afraid of so good a friend, for she is not insensible of kindness." A tear shone in Caroline's eye, as she

she handed her some sugar-plums and cakes she had brought in her pocket; and the little girl was the only one whose pleasure, at that time, was not mixt with regret. She was too young to feel her situation; and though she often found herself at a loss to express her meaning, she had not yet observed that others had not the same difficulty. But this was not the case with William, *he* severely felt the difference between himself and his brothers, though he could not understand what made it: he saw their lips move, and he moved his, unconscious whether he uttered a sound or not. In every other respect his senses were perfect, and perhaps more keen from this deficiency. Hardly any thing escaped

escaped his notice: he was even more useful to his mother than any of the rest, and whatever she wanted, he was the one most likely to find it out, and bring it to her, though he could not hear her say what it was. Her tears, as on this morning, were often mingled with her smiles, on observing his affectionate attention; and a sympathetic feeling would excite the same in him, though he could not judge from what cause it proceeded. He would wipe his eyes, and kiss the tears from hers, and then, with his arms around her neck, endeavour to comfort her with his inarticulate expressions. Happily for him, he was not conscious that the very attempt added to her distress.

He had this morning seen his mother's face enlivened by a smile, without any appearance of sorrow, and this was enough to make him happy. He had also seen his eldest brother preparing the cart to fetch their young visitors; and his memory, which was very retentive, immediately recurred to their former visits, in which he had often experienced their good-nature. Harry, the name-sake and foster-brother of little Rawlinson, was one year younger than he, but Wiliiam had long given up the seniority, and allowed him to take the lead in all their amusements. On seeing their guest, he recollected that the rabbits which he had often fed in Harry's absence, belonged to him, and pointing

ing to the place in which they were kept, endeavoured to draw him to them. The two Henrys immediately followed him; and Caroline was as eager to notice the baby Mrs. Goldsmith held in her arms. This again produced a sigh from the poor woman: "I am afraid," said she, "that this dear child is as unfortunate as my poor William and Lucy: it is now nine months old, and yet it does not seem to know its name. If I speak ever so loud, it does not turn its head, and I am very much afraid I shall never have the pleasure of hearing it answer me: only when it sees a thing, does it seem to notice it! Ah, my poor dear," continued she, "what shall I do with you?" "Oh, I hope you will not be so unfortunate, Mrs. Goldsmith," returned Caroline, and she again kissed the child and called it by its name. He saw her look of kindness, and smiled at her in return, but the sound of her voice did not reach him.

The servants, who had by this time unpacked the provision with which they were loaded, saw there was ground for the poor woman's fears, but Caroline would fain have persuaded her they were without foundation. The rest of Mrs. Goldsmith's family consisted of the boy who drove them, then about fourteen; Mary, the eldest girl, two years younger; and Jane, who was between Harry and little Lucy; a boy still younger, in petticoats; and

the

the little one in arms: seven in the whole; and three of these, my young readers, would have been incapable of getting their bread, had it not been for the Asylum I have spoken of: their parents being *poor*, and having no means of procuring for them such instruction as would make them useful, and which is provided for them there.

Master Goldsmith was a day-labourer, and at this time came home for his breakfast, which his cleanly wife had prepared for him before the company came: the bread and cheese and cold bacon were on the table when he entered. The kettle was also boiling, and all the party sat down to eat their meal together. Master Goldsmith and his eldest boy at one table, and the children and the maids, with Mrs. Goldsmith, at another. The little ones, who, on other mornings, had bread and milk for their breakfast, were on this occasion, treated with tea and bread and butter, as Mrs. Rawlinson had sent enough for all to partake of.

It was pleasing to see the attention which William paid to his sister Lucy: it seemed as if he considered her as doubly endeared to him, by their both sharing in the same misfortune; and yet those who noticed it were at a loss to account for his knowing it.—Nature had taught it him, and the sorrow of their mother was much alleviated by perceiving it. He watched every thing

thing that was given to her, and appeared more anxious that *she* should have enough, than for himself. When the rest of the children had had two cups of tea, and hers was not given to her immediately, he held up one of his fingers, (the way in which his mother had taught him to distinguish *numbers*,) and pointed to Lucy, as if to tell her she was neglected. Caroline saw his meaning, and touching his hand to draw his attention, offered him hers to give to his sister. With an eye as quick as lightning, he looked to his mother, as if to ask if that was proper, and seeing her disapprove, he shook his head, and again pointed to Lucy's cup, which, when Miller had once more filled, he nodded

ded his thanks, and quietly drank what was in his own. His father also was another object of his attention: he would have carried some tea to him, had not the good man preferred the more substantial food he was taking, and by signs made him understand so.

When the breakfast was ended, he and his son went again to their work; and Mary, after looking in vain to her mother, to introduce the subject for her, begged Miss Caroline to accept of a squirrel she had been taming purposely for her: "My brother made the cage, Miss," said she, "and you will be kind enough to excuse the rough work; but the little fellow in it, is what I hope you will like. William seemed

to

to know what she was speaking of; he watched her motions, and when he saw her bring the cage into the room, he discovered as much pleasure that he had understood what she intended to do with it, as that Miss Rawlinson should have it. He took some nuts out of his pocket, and showed her, those were what it was to eat; and then running to his mother, with a look which she as perfectly understood as if he had spoken to her, asked if she was not glad Miss Rawlinson was going to have it. But little Lucy, who had been often entertained by the squirrel's tricks, was not so willing it should be parted with: she thought something was going to be done with it, and, as well as she could, expressed

expressed her enquiries and dissatisfaction. William saw her distress, and by motions, understood only by themselves, made her know it was what *he* approved of, and if so, he concluded she could have no objection. In this conclusion he was right, for the countenance of Lucy immediately cleared up, and she appeared perfectly content.

After this, all the young ones, with Miller and Sally to take care of them, went to the copse to search for nuts; while Mrs. Goldsmith and her daughter staid within, to put away what had been used at breakfast, and to prepare the dinner. In the party out of doors, William was the most active: he climbed the trees, and not being interrupted by the

the conversation of the others, his whole attention was employed in gathering nuts for Miss Rawlinson and her brother, except that every now and then a glance was directed towards Lucy, who stood looking on his employment. With a look fully expressive of his meaning, he never presented the nuts to their visitors, without giving Lucy a few, as if to say: "Poor thing, she is but a child, and she is unfortunate; she will be uneasy if she has not some, and I know you will excuse it:" and then, with an approving nod and smile, he would direct her eyes towards their company, as if to make her sensible it was proper they should have the largest share. Having filled their little baskets, Miller prohibited

prohibited their gathering any more, and then proceeded to an opening in the middle of the wood, and agreed to play at *hunting the hare.* "And shall not William play with us?" said Caroline, as she was endeavouring to make him sensible of the game, while his brother Harry directed him to sit with Lucy at a distance. "I don't *like* that in *you*, Harry," said Henry Rawlinson, who thought he meant to forbid his joining them, "why should not he be amused as well as we?" Harry blushed, and said, "Lucy would not be quiet unless William was with her; besides, continued he, "when he sees what it is we are playing at, and can understand it, he will come; and he can make

Lucy

Lucy sit without him better than we can."

During this conversation, William had marked the countenance of each; he saw anger in that of Master Rawlinson, and shame in his brother's, and entirely unconscious that he was himself the cause, his whole attention was directed to make up the disagreement he perceived between them. Tears stood in his eyes as he took the hand of Harry, and bringing him to Henry, whom he thought he had offended, he stroked the face of each, and with an imploring look seemed to say: "Do be reconciled." "He *shall* play," said Henry. "My dear," said Miller, who now interfered, "he did not mean any other; but you must think that *he* knows best what will suit his brother." "*That's* what I meant," replied Harry, pleased to find some one take his part, "when he sees what our game is, he will join us." "So much the better then," said Henry; "I beg your pardon;" and taking the hand of his foster-brother, he gave it a hearty shake.

Smiles once more appeared in all their faces, but no countenance showed more pleasure than that of William, on seeing them thus friends again: he expressed it by nods, and winks, and wreathed smiles; and then went and took his place by Lucy, and in *his* manner made her understand they were going to play.

The game began, and the little girl

girl was as much amused by looking on, as they were who were engaged in it. She discovered no want of understanding, but clapped her hands and laughed as loud as any of them, fully entering into their amusement. When William became thoroughly acquainted with the game, he made her sensible he was going to join them, (as his brother had said he would,) and then Lucy was doubly interested. Whenever she saw *him* likely to be caught, she screamed out, not with alarm, but as if to warn him of his danger, though neither herself nor he could hear the caution.

During this pleasant exercise Mr. Beaufort arrived, to whom Henry had almost forgotten he had given pressing an invitation. The place of their retreat was near the road, and he heard the voices of his young friends, long before he saw them. Tying his horse to the paling which surrounded the house, he made his way to them, without seeing the good woman who belonged to it, and for some minutes he stood unobserved, till Henry Rawlinson caught his eye: "Oh, there is Mr. Beaufort!" said he, and the game was ended in an instant. The eyes of all were directed to the stranger, and William, who had not heard the exclamation, immediately saw the cause of their breaking off so abruptly; but indeed it was not particularly so to him, to whom, from not having his hearing, every thing

thing that happened, and for which he was not prepared by *seeing* what was going on, had that appearance. "You *are* come then," said Henry, to his friend, "this is very good of you;" and in his eagerness to welcome him, he had nearly overthrown little Lucy; who, on seeing the game ended, had risen from her seat to seek the hand of her favourite brother. "Oh, my dear!" said Henry, setting her again on her feet, "I did not mean to hurt you. She is deaf and dumb, Sir," continued he, addressing Mr. Beaufort, whose benevolent hand was stretched out to keep her from falling, and whose countenance, when he heard this, bore witness to his feelings. "Poor little girl," said he, offering her his

 hand,

hand, "what can be done for you?" Lucy looked half pleased, half frightened at his notice; yet there was something in his manner which excited her regard, and William's also, who by this time was at her side, and who read in the stranger's looks, that compassion for their case which he had often observed in others, when either Lucy or himself was the object of attention; and for which he felt a grateful sensation, such as seemed to tell him he had found a *friend.*

"And this poor boy has the same misfortune, Sir," said Miller, who was standing by them, and knowing the compassionate nature of Mr. Beaufort, felt assured he would not be unmindful of them. "Indeed!" replied

replied he, "and yet what intelligent faces." "Oh, Sir! they are both very sensible children," returned Miller, "and you would be delighted to see their affection for each other." "Have they never heard of the Asylum?" resumed Mr. Beaufort, with earnestness, "their misfortune might be greatly lessened.—Where is their mother? I'll speak to her about it;" and he turned hastily round, unmindful of his friend Henry, and every thing else but the charitable design he had in view. "She is within the house, Sir," answered Miller; "she feels their situation very keenly, but has no means of helping them." "I will help her," said he, as they led the way to the cottage. "There is one

one of our neighbour's sons in that Asylum," whispered Harry Goldsmith to his namesake, "and my mother has often wished William could be there; he has not been long, and he can speak already. She meant to ask your papa about it, the next time she came to town."

By this time Mr. Beaufort had entered the house; the table was neatly spread for the young folks' dinner, and the mother sitting with her baby in her arms. "Speak to it *now*, Mary," said she to her eldest daughter, who was standing behind, "*now* that it does not see you." She did so, but it took no notice. "Oh! at nine months old this would not be the case, if it was not deaf," continued the poor woman, with a heavy

heavy sigh. "Another unfortunate!" exclaimed Mr. Beaufort on hearing this, as he entered the door. Mrs. Goldsmith instantly arose, and Henry Rawlinson introduced him as a gentleman who had come from their house. "Set the gentleman a chair, Mary," said she; and while Lucy, who had now reached her mother's side, kept pulling her by the gown, and pointing towards the stranger, she motioned her to be silent; and rather seemed to wish her to escape his notice, than to obtrude her on his attention.

"I am come to know the state of your family, my good woman," said he, "and to know whether I can be of any service to you. How old is *that* little boy?" pointing towards

wards William. "Ten, Sir," answered she, "and the next is nearly eight." "No children older?" "Yes, Sir, a boy who is at work with his father, and that girl." "But whom do you wish assistance for most?" said Mr. Beaufort. "Oh, Sir, my poor William and Lucy!" she replied with great emotion; "they most need it." "I understand so," answered the benevolent man; "I know how they are situated; but do you know that there is a charity established lately, exactly suited to their case?" "Yes, Sir, I have heard of it," said she; "but I have no friend but Mr. Rawlinson," she continued, hesitatingly, "and I have thought that I would speak to him about it." "*I* will be your

your friend," said Mr. Beaufort; "I am one of the *governors* of that charity!"

It is impossible to describe the expression of joy and gratitude which appeared in the countenance of the poor woman. She could not utter a word; but her looks, and the tears which flowed from her eyes, spake her thanks more impressively than any thing she could have said. "No time is lost yet," continued Mr. Beaufort; "your boy could not have been admitted till he was nine years old, and, the next vacancy, I will give all my votes for him." The poor woman, a little recovered, could now express her thanks; and William, whose face had been like scarlet on seeing her distress, ad-

vanced

vanced towards her. "Have you taught him any thing?" asked Mr. Beaufort. "Oh, Sir, he has taught himself!" answered she, "he knows my meaning almost as soon as I look at him. I think he knows his *letters,* though I am not sure he puts the same meaning on them as we do; and figures he can tell, by counting on his fingers as many as he sees written. I am sure he does not want for sense, or his sister either; you can't think, Sir, how they love me, or how I love them! Dear little creatures, whenever I am out for a day's work, they sit by the road side together, and as soon as they see me, if it is at half a mile's distance, William leads little Lucy towards me, and they meet me with *such* delight!" "Why, my good woman," said Mr. Beaufort, whose eyes bore witness to the pleasure with which he heard her artless relation, "your other children will be jealous, if you thus speak of them." "No, they won't, Sir," said she, "they are very good; they know that I *ought* to love these best, because they are unfortunate. And this poor baby, Sir," added she, pressing it to her bosom, "I fear it is in the same state: it takes no notice of any thing but what it sees." "I am sorry for you," replied the good-natured man, "but we will hope better things: it may be only a temporary deafness. At present, this little boy is the most to be attended to;" and he took his

name

name and age down in his pocket-book, while the grateful mother put up a secret prayer that it might be attended with success.

William watched all that was done, with an expression of anxiety which could not be accounted for, unless he thought that something either very pleasant, or distressing, was to happen to his mother from it. The rest stood in silent attention, listening to what was said; and the countenance of each bespoke their earnest wishes for their brother's welfare.

Mr. Beaufort now invited Henry to ride with him to the spot Mr. Rawlinson had wished him to see; and Mrs. Goldsmith, seeing it was just one o'clock, pointed to the

door

door for William to go and call his father home to dinner. Lucy, who had been accustomed always to accompany him on that errand, made a sign to do so now; but William, by stepping out his feet in a peculiar manner, let her know that he must make great haste, and that she could not walk so fast as he; and with this information she was made satisfied to remain at home.

While Henry was riding before Mr. Beaufort, all their conversation was respecting William and the Asylum. "I will give all the money I have, for him to go," said the kind-hearted boy, "and I think that Caroline will too. I'll ask her when I get back." And on his return he called his sister on one side, to

 make

make the request: "Mr. Beaufort says that a great deal is wanting to support the children," said he, "and that they have built a new house for them to live in; the other was not large enough: won't you give *your* money towards it." "Yes, that I will;" replied she, "and as soon as we get home, we will speak to papa and mamma about it."

Mr. Beaufort had taken his leave, but not without a liberal earnest of his generosity to Mrs. Goldsmith, and an assurance that William should not be forgotten. He had brought his father and eldest brother home to dinner, to whom the poor woman related the circumstance of Mr. Beaufort's visit, with the greatest pleasure.

Never

Never was such a happy dinner as these affectionate parents sat down to with their young guests, though their feelings could scarcely allow either of them to partake of what was placed before them. "Why he'll speak as well as neighbour Goodyer's boy," said the delighted father, "*he* has been up to London to see him, and he says all the children are treated so kindly." "The time of admission is the second Monday in next month," said his mother, "and perhaps he may be admitted *then*. *We* are only expected to keep him decently clothed; I must begin making him some shirts; won't you let me buy him a few?" continued she. To this her husband readily consented; and Mil-

 ler

ler said she was sure her mistress would give him a jacket and trowsers. This point being settled, and the dinner ended, the children returned to their play, till the time of tea; after which, the horse was again harnessed to take them home, and the same party which he had brought in the morning, with the squirrel, and two rabbits Henry had obtained leave to take with him, were all placed in the cart, with a large basket of nuts, and some greens for the rabbits. They took their leave of nurse, with many thanks for the pleasure they had had, and expressions of kindness to all the children, particularly William and Lucy, the latter of whom had, in the course of the day, become so sociable with Caroline,

Caroline, as to cry at seeing her depart.

When they reached home, they found their parents, and Mr. Beaufort, sitting, after dinner, with another gentleman or two, and the little Goldsmiths were the subject of their conversation. Henry would have directly asked his mamma for his little store of money, that he might put it into Mr. Beaufort's hands, for the benefit of the charity, had not a significant look from Caroline prevented him. When they retired for the night, he asked her the reason. "It is like asking the gentlemen, who were strangers, to praise you," said she; "and besides, you know mamma has told us, that, whenever we give any thing away, we should not

not speak of it: to-morrow, when she is alone, will be time enough."

In a day or two after this, Mr. Beaufort returned to town, after fixing the day for William and his mother to come up, in time for the meeting, when he hoped to be so fortunate as to get him admitted. The intervening time was fully employed in preparing his clothes, in which Caroline assisted, and in endeavouring to make him understand the good fortune which awaited him. Mrs. Rawlinson had him to visit her, a day or two before he was to go; she took him to the school, to which, he recollected, his eldest brother had gone, and gave him a copy-book, pen and ink, and slate. William blushed, and lifting up his hand

hand affectingly, he shook his head, as if to say, "I don't know how to use them." He had been very fond of their neighbour's son, who was already in the Asylum, and before he went they were constant companions. William had for a long time understood he was gone somewhere greatly to his advantage, and whenever he went into the cottage of his parents, he pointed to the stool on which his old companion used to sit, as if to enquire how he was, while an approving smile from Mrs. Goodyer always told him he was well off.

On their return from Mrs. Rawlinson's, his mother took him to their neighbours, and directing his attention to the stool, which always recalled

recalled the idea of his friend, she showed him the books and slate which Mrs. Rawlinson had given him, and made him understand that he was gone to be instructed how to use them. William nodded his approval, but when she distinctly said, "*you* are to go *to* him," (and such a sentence as this he could understand by the motion of her lips,) he danced for joy, he kissed his mother and Mrs. Goodyer, caught up the books and hugged them, then the pen, with which he showed them he should soon know how to write; and then, by every means in his power, he asked the question *when* he should go? He looked up to the sky, then waved his hand with the sun, once, twice, thrice, as if

to

to enquire, was it in such a number of days? His mother held up one finger; and then, by moving his hand, as if in the act of driving, he asked if *that* was to be the mode of their conveyance. On receiving a nod of assent to this question also, he again capered round the room, and all the way, as they walked home, delighted his mother with his expressive gestures of pleasure.

When there, he met his brothers and sisters with increased affection, and with the same significant motions, made them sensible that he knew what was designed for him. He marked the return of the next evening with some appearance of regret, and, for the first time, seemed to recollect that all his family could not

not go with him; and he kissed them all again and again, especially little Lucy, who as yet had not a notion that she was so soon to lose him. He led her to his mother, and, with an expressive look, bespoke her double affection for her when he was away, and waving his hand towards the door, he tried to tell his sister he was going a great way off. In this manner he led her round to each of the family separately, as if to beg them all to be attentive to her in his absence.

The next morning, he and his mother were up before any of the children; and to spare him the pain of taking leave, she directed Mary not to awake them till they were gone. Our travellers had about a mile to walk to meet the coach, to which his father accompanied them, and, with the most earnest wishes for his success in gaining admittance, he bade his affectionate child—farewell.

Poor William had, till then, been all joy and ecstasy, but when he saw his father turning back, a tear stole from his eye. He had hoped, from his coming thus far with them, that *he* was also to accompany him; and with an enquiring look, he turned to his mother, with whom he was seated on the top of the coach, to know why he did not. The novelty of William's actions soon attracted the attention of the other passengers, and the recital of his case excited their pity. Among the number, the poor woman met with one who very well knew the part of the town she was going to, and where Mr. Beaufort had secured a room for them to sleep in, near the Asylum; and in the morning this benevolent man called to see her before the committee assembled. William instantly knew him again, and, from his mother's behaviour, he saw that it was to *him* he was obliged for the education he was about to receive, and with all the eloquence of silent gratitude he expressed his thanks.

At length eleven o'clock came, and William was introduced to the gentlemen. The votes were given, and he obtained his admission by a majority only of one; and that was from Mr. Beaufort having the number of votes which constitutes a governor

governor for life; and the pleasure with which he informed Mrs. Goldsmith of her son's success, could only be excelled by hers on hearing it.

William was then introduced to some of the scholars, among whom was Jacob Goodyer: they immediately recollected each other, and ran to express their pleasure in thus meeting. "How do you do, Mrs. Goldsmith?" said Jacob, delighted thus to use his newly-acquired speech, and to have an opportunity of displaying his improvement. "How are my father and mother?" The poor woman could not answer him: she burst into tears. "And will my boy ever speak so well as he?" she exclaimed to one

 of

of the matrons of the school, who was with her. "No doubt he will," answered the woman, who was equally affected. She then described more of Jacob's attainments; and when the first emotions of surprise were over, Mrs. Goldsmith was able to converse some time with him. He told her he had seen his father lately, begged her to carry his duty and love to all at home, and tell them he had made six pair of shoes since his father was there. He walked round the school and house with his old friends; told them how happy he was, and what pleasure it gave him that William was come, to whom he often spoke in his own way; and the poor boy, with the most intelli-

gent

gent look, showed how well he understood him.

Mr. Beaufort recommended Mrs. Goldsmith to stay one day longer in town, so that she had the pleasure of seeing her son happy, and settled in his new situation. He knew she was not to stay longer, and seemed reconciled to her departure; and before he gave her his parting kiss, he opened his book, and showed that he should be able to read and write by the time he saw her again; he also touched his mouth, in token that he should *speak*. She expressed her earnest hopes that it might be so, and, with the most affectionate regard, bade him be a good boy, and wished him farewell.

Jacob gave her a letter to carry

to his parents, the first he had ever written. And Mr. Beaufort, who was then in the house, promised that, if any thing happened to her son, she should immediately be informed of it; and also that, through Mr. Rawlinson's family, he would often let her know how he got on, and what improvements he made. With this assurance, the poor woman left him without the least regret, being well convinced that he was in the only place in which he could gain sufficient knowledge to become a useful member of society; and she returned to her expecting family, full of the kindness of the ladies and gentlemen she had met with, and the wonderful improvement of Jacob Goodyer, whose

parents

parents (particularly his mother) listened to her account with anxious joy. His letter was shown and read to all the village, as a proof of the excellency of the charity; and Mrs. Goldsmith received the congratulations of all her neighbours, on her son's being admitted into it.

It would be hardly possible to describe the distress of little Lucy, when she found her brother gone; nor was she old enough for them to make her understand it was for his advantage. She hunted in every part of the house and garden for him, and on not discovering the object of her search, she sat down and cried. Mary and Harry tried to pacify her, and with her dolls and playthings she began to be amused, till,

till, as the evening drew on, she put herself into a great bustle, and, taking Harry's hand, she led him to the road side, where, with William, she had so often sat, to watch the return of their mother. It was in vain he endeavoured to let her know she would not return that night, and Mary was at last obliged to put her crying to bed, where, at length, she forgot her sorrows in sleep. The next morning she renewed her search, and till her mother's return, she appeared truly unhappy; but on seeing her, her countenance revived, and while receiving *her* affectionate caresses, she seemed to forget that her brother was not returned with her.

Mr. Beaufort wrote frequent accounts

counts of William's welfare and improvements; and at the next vacation, to which all the family looked forward with pleasure, he was permitted to come home, with his neighbour Jacob Goodyer. They came on the top of the coach, and as they drew near their home, these poor boys expressed to each other the greatest pleasure. "I shall *speak* to my mother," said William, and hardly had he spoke the words, than he saw her standing with Lucy, Harry, and Jane, who had all walked a mile or two to meet him. The agitation he felt, at thus unexpectedly seeing them before he reached home, prevented his speaking as he wished: he pulled the coachman's arm, and pointing to the happy group below, his

his lips moved, but he could not utter a word. The coach stopped, and he was down in an instant, and in his mother's arms. "Mother! my dear mother!" repeated he, as articulately as his emotion would allow him, while Harry and Jane were in raptures to hear his voice.

Jacob had yet some miles further to go; he could therefore only nod and smile, rejoicing that, in a very short time, he should have a pleasure equal to his friend's. "We will go round by the field where your father is at work, my dear," said the delighted mother, "for he is impatient to see you." "My father," returned William, "and Edward," meaning his eldest brother. He then repeated the names of all his brothers

thers and sisters, and received the affectionate welcome of those who were then present. Lucy did not at first recollect him; but when he spoke to her, and she observed his looks and motions, no one can express her pleasure. She kissed him twenty times, pressed his hand, and held it tight all the way they walked together, as if nothing should again part them from each other.

When they reached their father, William ran towards him, and repeating his name, made the heart of the poor man leap for joy: "Oh, my dear boy!" said he, "*do* you speak at last?" Well, if I lose some of my week's wages, I must leave work, and go home with you. Here, Edward, Edward," continued he, calling

ing to his eldest son, who was in the next field, "William is come home." Edward heard the news with pleasure, and impatient to see the brother for whom they were so deeply interested, he jumped over the hedge in an instant;, and William no sooner saw him, than he flew to meet him, and greeted him with all the expressions of joy which he could utter. This was a happy evening for them all, and when the joyful party arrived at the cottage, Mary, who had been left in charge of the baby, expressed the same delight.

The tea-things were ready, and William repeated the names of every thing he saw; he walked round the room, and, as if anxious to show the advantage he had gained, called over all

all that was in it, or on the shelves about the room, while his delighted parents listened with fond emotion to all he said. His little stock of clothes was now opened, and eagerly taking out his spelling-book, which was in the parcel, he began to read. He showed his writing also; in short, there was none of his acquirements which he was not eager to exhibit, and to receive the congratulations of his parents upon. He watched the motion of their lips, and understood every word they said, when they expressed their pleasure to each other.

In the course of the next day, he visited his old acquaintance in the village, whither little Lucy accompanied him, proud to be once more with her dear brother. All the neighbours were astonished at his improvement, and William was in danger of thinking himself something extraordinary, he was so much noticed and admired. He also paid his respects to Mrs. Rawlinson; and received from her the sincerest congratulations, as well as from his old friends, Miller and Sally. Caroline and Henry made him say every thing that he could speak; and when unable to answer them, (which, among the numerous questions they asked him, was sometimes the case,) they immediately removed the distress he showed on these occasions, by replying for him. Yet this did not seem to satisfy him, and before he left them, he was, after repeatedly endeavouring,

endeavouring, able to pronounce the word himself.

A few days after this, Jacob Goodyer came over to visit his friend, and it was pleasant to see with what delight they met each other. The simplicity of childhood was blended with their artless manners, and they seemed to take an interest in each other's concerns, which none other could have. William related to his attentive friend, all that had happened to him since they parted; even mentioned what he had ate and drank each day, and received the same information from Jacob. While thus conversing with each other, they seemed to feel themselves the objects of attention to all around; but when they could get away together,

 quite

quite alone, and enjoy a conversation in their own way, partly by signs mingled with words, (for though able to understand others by the motion of their lips, *they* could not so exactly frame *their* mouths to pronounce what they wished, as to be clearly comprehended by the *sight* alone,) it appeared as if nothing was wanting to their happiness.

Each of these unfortunate children, throughout the whole school, seemed allied to the others by a nearer tie than that of relationship: they were a world within themselves, and their manners and ideas were, in one sense, unmixed with that evil which is in others. Having not the sense of hearing, their acquaintance with what was wrong was

was excluded through this channel; and as, before their admittance to the school, their age and misfortune in great measure precluded their beholding it; so, while they were there, the attention paid to their morals, and to keep them from every thing which might add to that taint of sin, which is so inherent in our nature, and which these children were not exempt from, gave to the simplicity with which they acted, the appearence of innocence; or rather what is called so by us, who are totally ignorant of what *innocence* really is, and can only comparatively judge of it. They were taught to love each other, and feeling themselves equally unfortunate, there was not among them that air of superiority, which too many are apt to assume. from possessing powers which they see are wanting in others. The pride, also, of the human heart, revolts at times at the compassion shown in such cases, though at others it feels grateful for the expression of it, and much depends on the manner in which it is displayed; but among themselves there was nothing of this sort—all felt for each other. Their wants they could often make known to others; but while shut out from the power of language, they could not describe their comforts to any one, so well as to themselves.

William and Jacob both spake highly of the school, and of the kindness with which they were treated;

ed; and, as the time for their going back drew near, they rather expressed pleasure than regret at the thought of returning. Mrs. Goldsmith bade her boy farewell, with still greater comfort than at the first; she was now assured of his improvement, and had no fear of his continuing to do so. Jacob had tried to persuade him to become a shoe-maker like himself, at which employment he was getting more and more expert; but William had always shown a desire to be a cabinet maker, and the gentleman of the committee meant to indulge him in having him instructed in that trade, making it a point to consult the disposition of the children, where it was possible.

In

In the course of the next half year, Mr. Beaufort paid a second visit to Mr. Rawlinson; and while there, kindly called on Mrs. Goldsmith, with the pleasing intelligence of William's advancement both in speaking, writing, and the business which he was now learning. The poor woman thanked him for his goodness, while he enquired after Lucy and the youngest child, who was now two years old, and the fears of his mother unfortunately confirmed, as it evidently appeared he was a sharer in the affliction which attended the others. Mr. Beaufort gave her hopes, that, as the fund increased, the scheme would be enlarged, and that he should then have it in his power to get one or both of of them into the school, when they were of a proper age.

"I hope they will," said Henry Rawlinson, who had accompanied his old friend, (not now riding before him, as when they first met at the cottage, but on a little horse his father had bought for him,) "I hope they will: it is such an advantage to William, that I should be sorry the others should not share it likewise. And Jacob Goodyer, also, will be able to get his living any where; his father says he will soon come home, and make shoes for the whole parish." Mr. Beaufort smiled at this information, and, as they returned, Henry enquired if the fund did not increase. "I wish I was a man," said he; "I would give a great deal

deal towards it." "My dear boy," said Mr. Beaufort, "you give a great deal now, for your age;" (for Henry and Caroline also, had, from their first hearing of this charity, contrived to lay by part of their pocket-money towards the support of it;) "if every boy and girl were to spare as much from their weekly or quarterly allowance as you do, and your sister, how would the fund be increased, as well as the pleasure they would receive from thus employing it. Perhaps three or four children might be admitted every year, in addition to the present number; and thus they might be a means of rescuing their fellow-creatures from a state worse than that of oblivion!" "Oh, that they would!" said Henry, ready

ready to spring from his horse at the idea; "Oh, that they would! and did they but know the pleasure it gave to poor nurse Goldsmith to hear her son speak, I think there would be no doubt of it."

We shall now proceed to relate the further benefit this benevolent institution was to William, and how it enabled him, in some measure, to requite the kindness of Mr. Beaufort and Henry Rawlinson, as well as materially to assist his family when he grew up.

When Mr. Beaufort returned to town, he took Henry with him for a fortnight's pleasure, and knowing it would be as great a one to him as any, to see William Goldsmith, and the manner in which he was instructed,

instructed, almost the first place they visited, was the Asylum in which he was placed. He saw the method by which these unfortunate children were taught to speak—the kind attention of their teachers—the way in which they lived—and how they were permitted to amuse themselves. William had great pleasure in speaking to him of these things, and that Henry might carry the most accurate account of himself and his proceedings to his mother, he showed him every part of the school, as well as of his workmanship, from which the governors permitted him to send her a small trifle of his own making.

During the time Henry staid with Mr. Beaufort, as a further pleasure

to

to them both, William was one day asked to dine; and after dinner, as Henry expressed a wish to walk out, Mr. Beaufort gave him leave, and William to accompany him. The two boys set off together, highly delighted, and Henry made William understand that he would go and look at the Monument. He had been there once with Mr. Beaufort, but he wished to see it again; and he thought he knew the way: "if not," said he, "I can enquire, and what harm can happen to us?" William was equally pleased with his intention; but before they had proceeded far on their way, so many various things in the different shop-windows attracted their attention, and the crowds of people who were continually passing, with the narrowness of the steets, all added to the difficulty they had in keeping with each other; and at length, in crossing the road, they were entirely separated. William had been standing at a shop-window, and who, from his want of hearing, had been more used to have his eyes employed, did not cross so soon as Henry, as he saw some carriages in the way; but he hoped to find his friend waiting for him on the other side. How was he disappointed, therefore, on not finding him there. He looked on every side, but could see no one like him; he walked on a little way, then back again, fearing he might have passed him in the crowd; till, at a distance, and on the opposite

side

side of the way, he saw two men bearing in their arms a boy of his size, and who appeared to be lifeless. Judge of his alarm and distress, when, on pushing by the carriages, and hastening towards them, he saw it was Henry himself, whom they were thus carrying. He followed them into one of the narrow lanes or alleys, with which London abounds; and saw them take him into a low, dirty-looking house, into which he entered also. "He is not much hurt," said they, not at all attending to William's being there; "only stunned a little: he is a gentleman's son, I can see, by his clothes, and if we keep him here, he will be advertised, and we shall get a handsome reward." "*I* know who he is," is," said William; *I* know to whom he belongs," as articulately as his agitation would allow him to speak. "Hollo!" said one of the brutish fellows, "who have we here? a dumb boy! Don't let us mind what *he* says, he may be a *fool* for what we know."

It was well for Henry, and William also, perhaps, that the distress he felt, prevented his speaking more distinctly at that time; for had they found that he could have been understood, they would have kept *him* there also, in order to conceal the place that Henry was in; from the hope, that the longer his parents were kept in suspense about him, the larger reward would be offered. But supposing that William's information

formation would be unintelligible, or considered of no consequence, they forced him from the house; and he had the distress of seeing that Henry had not recovered his senses, when he was thus obliged to leave him.

He ran back to Mr. Beaufort's, with all the speed he was capable of using, feeling what none can enter into but those who are in a similar situation—a dread of the danger his friend was in; anticipating the distress, if not the displeasure, of Mr. Beaufort: and, above all, afraid that he should not be able to speak so as to be understood. Almost out of breath, and with a face pale and full of distress, he rapped at the door. "What is the matter?" said the

the footman who opened it, alarmed at his countenance; but William could only answer by his tears. On hearing this, Mr. Beaufort, who was still sitting with his wine after dinner, hastened out of the parlour, and seeing only William, immediately guessed the cause of his distress. "You have lost Henry," said he; "I was foolish to let you go out together." William tried in vain to speak, but pulling him by the arm, he waved his hand for Mr. Beaufort to accompany him. The good man caught up his hat, and telling the footman to follow, he hastened, with the trembling boy, to the place in which he had left Henry. "Has any accident happened?" said Mr. Beaufort, looking steadily at William,

William, who could only shake his head; till being a little recovered, he endeavoured to acquaint him with what he had seen. Mr Beaufort hurried on, and they were presently at the house.

The man who opened the door, on seeing William with the gentleman, thought it would be of no use to deny Henry's being there, he therefore expressed pleasure, rather than surprise, at seeing him; and said, "we have taken great care of the young gentleman, Sir, and he is better already." "Have you sent for a surgeon?" asked Mr. Beaufort; "let me see him directly," and rushing forward, he discovered Henry lying on an old blanket upon the floor, with a bundle of rags for his pillow.

pillow. His eyes were open, and he instantly knew the friends who were about him. William wept for joy at again seeing him sensible, while Mr. Beaufort, with great indignation, exclaimed: "Do you call *this* taking care of him?" "Bless your honour," replied the man, "we are but poor folk, and have no better place; but my wife is gone out to see if she can get a bed for him."

This was a made-up story, and William, by his countenance, showed he thought it so. Mr. Beaufort having sent his servant for a surgeon, he asked if there was not a chair in the house, in which Henry might be placed, for none was in the room. The man brought in a very

very old one, and with his assistance Mr. Beaufort lifted him into it. "A carriage knocked him down, your honour." said the man, "but it did not go over him; and I and my comrade took him up. We did not know to whom he belonged." "And where was *you* at this time?" asked Mr. Beaufort, turning to William. "Oh, Sir," said he, now quite able to speak, "I was looking in at a shop-window, and I did not see the accident; but I saw the men with him in their arms, and saw them bring him here. I told them that I knew who he was, and where he lived, but they would not hear me." "We did not know what he said, your honour," replied the man, with a still more servile air, "and we could not

not think that such a one as he could tell us any thing about the young gentleman."

William watched every word the man spoke, and, with his eyes flashing fire, he replied: "But *I* knew what *you* said, and I believe you understood me, though you pretended not; for you said that you would not attend to what I told you, and that he was a gentleman's son, and that a handsome reward would be offered for him; and you would not let me stay with him, but pushed me out of doors." Mr. Beaufort saw, by the man's countenance, that he understood William, and with a significant look, he said, "you may depend upon it that you shall be *rewarded,* and that all the accommodation

tion the *young gentleman* has had shall be paid for."

At this moment the surgeon arrived, who pronounced the patient to be in no danger, but that it was necessary for him to be bled. This was immediately done, after which a chair was procured, and the invalid, who already declared himself much better, was taken home, Mr. Beaufort and William walking all the way with the chairmen.

Before they left the house, Mr. Beaufort offered the man half-a-crown:—"Quite as much as you deserve," said he, "for it is clear, had it been in your power, you would have kept his friends in ignorance of his situation, till they had enquired for him; nor would you have let

let them know it then, till their anxiety had led them to pay a good price for the information. And as for your wife's being gone to seek a bed for him, I don't believe a word of it." The man began to grumble at the smallness of the sum; he declared he had lost half a day's work by it, and if he had known he should have had such a *small* matter for it, he would have let him lie there till that time. "I readily believe it," said Mr. Beaufort; "but remember, you are in *my* power, and if you are at all abusive, I know how to procure a constable. This boy's evidence, or mine either, will not be much in your favour. I know how to reward assistance, but not imposition; and I can distinguish what is *servile* from civility."

On

On their getting home, Henry was put to bed, and William sat by him till it was time for him to return to the Asylum; but never did he go towards it with such regret. To have remained with Henry all night would have been the highest gratification he could at that time have had; however, he had the pleasure of leaving him *well*, in comparison to the state he had seen him in, and in the care of a kind friend; and with these thoughts, and the comparison of what his feelings would have been had he not discovered him as he did, he endeavoured to reconcile himself to returning.

The next day he was afraid to ask leave to go out again, as it was not a holiday; but when he was at liberty, he narrowly watched the entrance into the yard, hoping that every person who came into it might be Mr. Beaufort, or some one from his house, from whom he could gain some information respecting Henry. But, alas! no one arrived, and his anxiety increased as the day declined. At length he thought of sending a note to Mr. Beaufort, and getting one of the elder scholars to write it for him, he set forth, with the most affecting simplicity, his uneasiness at not hearing of Henry; he begged his pardon for being thus troublesome; "but," continued he, "I do so want to know how Master Rawlinson is, that if you could tell me he was *well*, it seems as if I should want nothing else."

Mr.

Mr. Beaufort smiled at his expression; but he could not be angry, except with himself, that he had not thought of letting him know that his friend was recovering very fast; and the next morning Henry was well enough to accompany him to the Asylum, where William had the pleasure of once more beholding him, and *seeing* him say he felt no ill effects from the accident, that had so alarmed him; but the part which he had taken in it, and his letting Mr. Beaufort know into what hands he had fallen, was not easily erased from the mind of Henry, and he expressed his sense of it in strong terms. "The Asylum," said he, "has been an advantage to *me*, for if William had not been educated there, I should have had no one to speak for me when I was senseless, and no one would have known to whom I belonged." "Did I not say, your beneficence would not go unrewarded?" said Mr. Beaufort, exultingly; "and if you never meet with a similar occurrence, *this* has been sufficient to convince you that such a way of disposing of your money has not been useless."

And *thus*, I hope, will some of my readers think, and, as far as is in their power, contribute their little share towards the support of such an institution. Let them reflect, that though such a circumstance as I have described may never happen, yet the enabling these poor children to understand, and be understood;

stood; the relieving their parents from the anxiety they must feel on their account, while in the helpless state their misfortune places them in; as well as removing what they themselves would have felt, on being all their lives useless and a burden to others, are no mean advantages; and, to some minds, these would be more powerful inducements, than the chance of its being a benefit to themselves.

On his return home, Henry related this adventure to his old friend and nurse, Mrs. Goldsmith, with the most grateful sensations; who, in her turn, rejoiced that her son had been of such service to one whom she so loved. Caroline received equal pleasure on hearing of her brother's escape; and from this time, not only the annual gift of the young folk to the charity was increased, but that of their parents also.

William was always considered as more peculiarly their charge, and each time he came home, while in the school, he was well clothed by Mrs. Rawlinson, in remembrance of the service he had done her son. All their interest was also exerted to get his sister Lucy into the Asylum, who, from the instructions he had given her when at home in the vacations, was much forwarder in her education when she went there, than he was; and at her return from it, she was able to get her living by needle-work. Most of her employment is in Mrs. Rawlinson's family,

and

and those to whom she recommends her. William works as a journeyman cabinet-maker and upholsterer, having now perfectly learned the trade; and is enabled to add greatly to the comforts of his family, as well as procure for himself every necessary of life. Jacob Goodyer also set up the trade of shoe-making when he returned home, and, as his delighted father had said, was employed by the whole parish. These young men retain a particular friendship for each other, and no pleasing occurrence which happens to one, is half so gratifying, if not shared by the other. The part which they take in each other's feelings, can only be compared to that interest, which men, belonging to the same society,

society, feel for each other in a distant country, where, though they may meet with attention and kindness from the inhabitants of it, they are still considered as strangers, and the union among themselves is strengthened by it.

His youngest brother has a particular claim to William's attention; and Mr. Beaufort, who has by no means forsaken the family, promises to use his interest in assisting him, as he already has his brother and sister; but so many are the candidates on the list at present, whose circumstances are still more distressing*, that, unless the fund increases

* See the list at the end, copied from the account of this charity.

so as to admit a larger number, Mrs. Goldsmith herself can hardly wish his success, when she reflects what must be the feelings of many of those mothers, who have travelled more than once or twice to town with their children, and received the severe disappointment of their not being admitted from want of room. Such, the author knows, has been the case of many; and again she recommends it to her readers to consider whether it is not in their power to add a small sum—if ever so little, *that* willingly, and regularly bestowed, might at least save *one* of these anxious mothers another disappointment. Would every one who reads this book, but ask their acquaintance to join their little to their own, (supposing

(supposing it was only what they would spend one morning in the week at the pastry-cook's,) this added together would make no inconsiderable sum in the list of donations; and a lasting benefit would accrue to their unfortunate fellow-creatures of the same age, and with the same feelings as themselves, and who, like them, have to pass through this world, perhaps to spend many years in it. But, alas! unless the advantage of this charity be extended to them, these years must be spent in sorrow, or unmeaning cheerfulness, and without the means of improvement either to the mind or body.

EXTRACT

FROM THE

ACCOUNT OF THE CHARITY,

IN 1809.

"In order to acquaint the public with the unfortuuate condition of these mute supplicants of benevolence, a few of the cases now in the Asylum are subjoined.

"William Coleman, mother a widow, with eleven children; five deaf and dumb.

"Anne Coleman, parents poor working people, eight children; five deaf and dumb.

"Matthew Thistle, father has six children; three deaf and dumb.

"Mary Cannon, father poor, five children; three deaf and dumb.

"Samuel Gosling, parents paupers, three children; all deaf and dumb.

"Mary Everitt, father a labourer, seven girls; two deaf and dumb.

"Joseph Tuck, six children, orphans; three deaf and dumb.

"Henry Willisee, father and mother deserted their family; two deaf and dumb.

"Jacob Marret, father poor, six children; two deaf and dumb.

"William Willisee, father at sea; another deaf and dumb.

"William Sharp, father a journeyman miller; nine children.

"Richard Chatband, father a victualler; seven children.

"Elizabeth Thorne, father a dissenting minister; six children.

"Mary Anne Hooker, father a journeyman chandler; six children.

"Edward Harper, father a dissenting minister; five children.

"Thomas Dean, father a victualler; five children.

"Jane Garwood, father a pauper; five children.

"Elizabeth Cooper, mother a char-woman; five children.

THE END.

Printed by Darton, Harvey, and Co.
Gracechurch-Street, London.

BOOKS FOR YOUTH,

PUBLISHED BY

DARTON, HARVEY, AND DARTON,

Gracechurch-Street, London.

ORIGINAL POEMS for INFANT MINDS, by several young Persons, two Vols, half bound, Price 3*s*.

"We have seldom seen a book, the title of which has so well corresponded with the contents. The poetry is very superior to what is usually found in books of this kind, and the moral tendency of the whole is excellent." *Imperial Review.*

RHYMES for the NURSERY, by the Authors of Original Poems, Price 1*s* 6*d*. half bound.

"We have not room for extracts, or could convince our readers, that the writers of these 'Rhymes,' have better claims to the title of poets, than many who arrogate to themselves that high appellation." *Critical Review.*

RURAL SCENES; or a Peep into the Country, for Good Children; illustrated by nearly One Hundred Cuts, with appropriate descriptions in Prose and Verse. By the Authors of Original Poems. Price 2*s*. 6*d*. neatly half bound.

CITY SCENES; or a Peep into London, for Good Children, by the Authors of Rural Scenes. With 103 Copper-plates. Price 2*s*. 6*d*. half bound.

LIMED TWIGS, to catch Young Birds, by one of the Authors of Original Poems. Price 2*s*. half bound.

A

THE WEDDING among the FLOWERS, by one of the Authors of Original Poems. With Plates. Price 1*s*.

HYMNS FOR INFANTS, by the Authors of Original Poems. Price 1*s*. 6*d*. half bound.

KNOWLEDGE FOR INFANTS; or, a Form of Oral Instruction, for the Use of Parents and Teachers By A. Lindley Price 1s.

THE NEW CHILDREN'S FRIEND; or, Pleasing Incitements to Wisdom and Virtue, conveyed through the Medium of Anecdote, Tale, and Adventure: calculated to entertain, fortify, and improve the juvenile Mind. Translated chiefly from the German. Sixth Edition. Price 2s. half bound.

THE DECOY; or, an agreeable Method of teaching children the elementary Parts of English Grammar, by Conversations and familiar Examples. Price 1*s*.

SCRIPTURAL STORIES; for very young Children. By the Author of the Decoy. Price 1*s*.

JULIA and the Pet Lamb; or, Good-nature and Compassion rewarded. By the Author of the Decoy. Price 1*s*.

THE RATIONAL BRUTES; or, Talking Animals. By M. Pelham. Price 1*s*. 6*d*.

The Rational Brutes and Talking Animals, to which this book relates, are no other than an assembly of imaginary creatures, of different species: viz. dogs, horses, cats, &c. are supposed by the author, to relate in human language, the cruelties inflicted upon each of them by thoughtless and ill-natured children; of which such animals would doubtless complain were they endued with reason and speech. To be a tongue to the dumb, in such a cause, is a praiseworthy act; and we hope the benevolent advocate of the brute creation, has not pleaded their cause in vain."---*Guardian of Education.*

Published by Darton, Harvey, and Darton.

A COMPENDIOUS HISTORY OF THE WORLD, from the Creation to the Dissolution of the Roman Republic. By John Newbery. With a Continuation to the Peace of Amiens, 1802. In two vols. 18mo. with engraved Frontispieces, 5*s.* in boards.

This is a useful book for young persons. "It is very neatly printed; and is very cheap. It is a very conspicuous compendium, and the style is good and easy."—*British Critic, October.* 1804.

THE NEWTONIAN SYSTEM OF PHILOSOPHY, explained by familiar Objects, in an entertaining manner for the Use of Young Persons. By T. Telescope, A.M. A new improved Edition, with many Alterations and additions, to explain the new Philosophical Discoveries. Price 2*s.* half bound.

GEOGRAPHY MADE EASY for CHILDREN; with an Appendix, containing a short and familiar Account of the principal new Discoveries. By *John Newbery.* The Third Edition, improved and adapted to the Modern Divisions of Europe; Illustrated with Plates and Maps. Price 3s.. bound.

AUNT MARY'S TALES, for the Entertainment and Improvement of little Boys. Addressed to her Nephews. Price 2*s.* half bound.

DOMESTIC REREATION; or Dialogues illustrative of Natural and Scientific Subjects. By *Priscilla Wakefield.* Two vols. Price 5*s.*

Books for Youth.

MORAL VIEWS; or, the Telescope, for Children, illustrated with Four Copper-plates, a new Edition. Price 2*s*. 6*d*.

"The various lessons of virtue, which are inculcated in this little volume, are well adapted to improve the morals, and to cherish the benevolent feelings of young persons. They will find in his collection, invitations to industry and application, to an open and ingenuous conduct, to a taste for simple pleasures, to humanity, and to piety."
Monthly Review, Sept. 1805.

INCIDENTS OF YOUTHFUL LIFE; or, the History of William Langley. The Fourth Edition. Price 1*s*. 6*d*. half bound.

THE JUVENILE SPEAKER; or Dialogues and Miscellaneous Pieces, in Prose and Verse, for the Improvement of Youth in the Art of Reading, &c. Price 2s. half bound.

SCENES FOR THE YOUNG; or, Pleasing Tales, calculated to promote good Manners and the love of Virtue. By *I Day*. Price 1*s*. 6*d*. half bound.

"These tales are correct and useful in point of moral tendency; they are also written with care and intelligence. We would encourage the same author to resume his pen, advising him constantly to keep in view the developement of some useful maxim, and also the introduction of some interesting information."
Eclectic Review, April, 1807.

OUTLINES OF ENGLISH HISTORY, in Verse. By *Elizabeth Rowse*. Price 2*s*. half bound.

THE MOTHER'S FABLES, in Verse, designed, through the Medium of Amusement, to convey to the Minds of Children some useful Precepts of Virtue and Benevolence. Price 1*s*. 6*d*. half bound.

VERSES for CHILDREN. Written by a young Lady for the Amusement of her little Brothers and Sisters. Price 6*d*.

www.ingramcontent.com/pod-product-compliance
Ingram Content Group UK Ltd.
Pitfield, Milton Keynes, MK11 3LW, UK
UKHW020210080825
7288UKWH00055B/429

9 781021 344779